Once There Was A Bull... (frog)

By Rick Walton

Illustrated by Greg Hally

Salt Lake City

02 01 00 99   10 9 8 7 6 5 4

Published by
Gibbs Smith, Publisher
P.O. Box 667
Layton, Utah 84041

Book design by Traci O'Very Covey

Printed and bound in Hong Kong

Library of Congress Cataloging-in-Publication Data

Walton, Rick.
Once there was a bull--frog / written by Rick Walton; illustrated by Greg Hally.--1st ed.
p. cm.
Summary: A bullfrog in the Old West loses his hop in this lively tale where each page must be turned to complete the previous image.
ISBN 0-87905-652-5
[1.Frogs--Fiction.] I.Hally, Greg, ill. II. Title
PZ7.W17740n 1995   94-32513
[E]--dc20   CIP
AC

Dedicated

to Carolee and Terry Ferris
and all their little hoppers
— R.W.

to Daddy's girls, Lauren and Madison
— C.H.

Once there was a **bull**...

frog who had lost his hop.

He looked under a **toad**...

stool. But his hop wasn't there.

He looked behind a **dog**...

house. But his hop wasn't there.

He looked under a hedge...

hog. But his hop wasn't there.

"Maybe if I jump off something I'll find my hop,"
he said, so he climbed on top of a **box**...

car and jumped!

He landed hard in a patch of **grass**...

hoppers. They hopped away, but Bullfrog didn't.

"Not high enough," said Bullfrog. "Maybe if someone threw me, I'd go high enough to get my hop back."

"I'll do it," said a **cow**...

boy, who loved to throw things, and he picked up Bullfrog and tossed him high and far.

Bullfrog tumbled through the air
and landed in a field of **straw**...

berries. "Oof!" Then he tried to hop.
He couldn't. "Oh, woe," said Bullfrog. "I've lost my hop!"

"Then swim," said a **cat**...

fish from the stream nearby.
"I can't swim on land," said Bullfrog.

"Then fly," said a **lady**...

bug who heard Bullfrog complain. "I can't," said Bullfrog. "I have no wings. And without wings, flying hurts."

"You could *slither*," said a voice behind Bullfrog.
He turned and looked.
On the ground behind him was a **diamond**...

back rattlesnake looking for breakfast.
"A snake!" croaked Bullfrog.

And up into the air he leaped, higher than the **sun**…

flowers around him. And when he came down, he leaped again. And again. And again.

Until he landed on a *stage*...

coach. "I've found it! I've found my hop!" said Bullfrog as he rode out of town and far from the snake.

"And after all that hopping, I'm so hungry
I could eat a **horse**...

fly!" And he did.